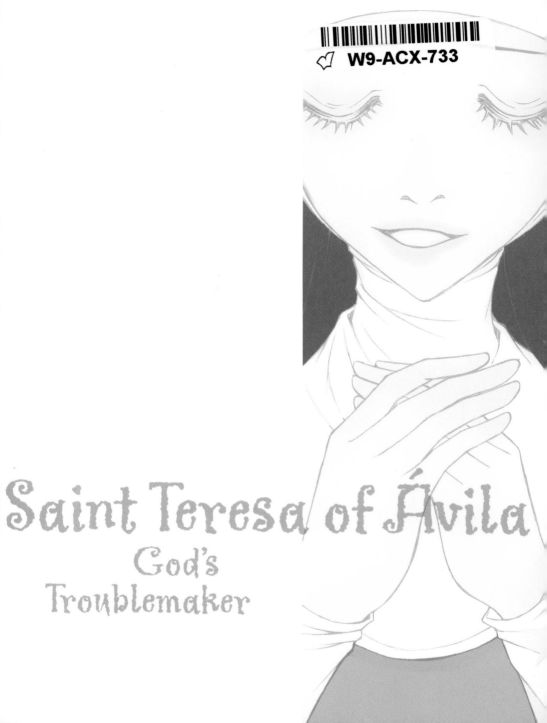

Saint Teresa of Ávila
God's
Troublemaker

Saint Teresa of Ávila

God's Troublemaker

Written and Illustrated by Yoon Song-i

Pauline
BOOKS & MEDIA
Boston

Library of Congress Cataloging-in-Publication Data

Yun, Song-i.
  [Abilla ui songnyo T'eresa. English]
  Saint Teresa of Avila : God's troublemaker / by Yoon Song-i ; translated by the Kate Yoon.
     pages cm
  ISBN 978-0-8198-9038-2 -- ISBN 0-8198-9038-3
  1. Teresa, of Avila, Saint, 1515-1582. 2. Christian saints--Spain--Avila--Biography. I. Title.
  BX4700.T4Y8613 2014
  282.092--dc23
  [B]
                            2014012578

아빌라의 성녀 데레사 (Saint Teresa of Ávila) by YOON Song-i

© 2010 by YOON Song-i, www.pauline.or.kr.

Originally published by Pauline Books & Media, Seoul, Korea. All rights reserved.

Translated by Kate Yoon

Published by Pauline Books & Media, 50 Saint Pauls Avenue, Boston, MA 02130–3491

Printed in the U.S.A.

STAGT VSAUSAPEOILL3-510112 9038-3

www.pauline.org

Pauline Books & Media is the publishing house of the Daughters of St. Paul, an international congregation of women religious serving the Church with the communications media.

3 4 5 6 7 8 9   22 21 20 19 18

Contents

THAT'S THE WAY TO FIND THE MOORS FROM AFRICA* . . .

LET'S GO, RODRIGO! IF WE DIE AS MARTYRS—AT THE HANDS OF THE MOORS—WE'LL GET TO SEE GOD RIGHT AWAY!

*THE MOORS WERE MUSLIMS FROM NORTH AFRICA. THE MOORS WANTED TO SPREAD THEIR FAITH IN EUROPE. CHRISTIANS WHO DEFENDED THEIR FAITH OR TRIED TO CONVERT THE MOORS TO CHRISTIANITY KNEW THAT THEY WERE RISKING THEIR LIVES.

2

HERE, RODRIGO, EAT SOME OF THE BREAD I BROUGHT FOR OUR TRIP . . .

GRAB

GOTCHA, YOU RASCALS!!

COME ON, LET'S GET YOU BOTH HOME. YOUR MAMÁ IS REALLY WORRIED ABOUT YOU.

BUT TÍO, WE *WANT* TO GO TO AFRICA.

OH! TÍO!*

WHAT WERE YOU THINKING? RUNNING AWAY FROM HOME?? WE'VE BEEN SEARCHING FOR YOU SINCE THIS MORNING!

GRUMBLE GRUMBLE

AFRICA? WHY IN THE WORLD DO YOU WANT TO GO TO AFRICA? YOU DON'T EVEN KNOW HOW FAR AFRICA IS FROM ÁVILA, SPAIN.

*TÍO IS SPANISH FOR UNCLE.

3

WHEW . . . I JUST DON'T KNOW WHAT TO DO WITH THESE CHILDREN. THEY WERE SO MOVED BY THE STORIES YOU READ TO THEM

ABOUT MARTYRS DYING AT THE HANDS OF THE MOORS. THAT'S WHY THEY WERE RUNNING AWAY TO AFRICA.

WHAT?! MY CHILDREN WERE TRYING TO BECOME MARTYRS AT THE HANDS OF THE MOORS?

아하하하

HA HA HA!

THIS IS *YOUR* FAULT! BECAUSE YOU READ ALL THOSE BOOKS TO THEM, THEY WANT TO DO THE SAME AND SEE GOD RIGHT AWAY!

BETTER THAN STORIES ABOUT KNIGHTS.

흐응... 꽃미남 기사라니...

WELL, AT LEAST I DON'T READ THEM CHEESY LOVE STORIES ABOUT PRINCESSES FALLING IN LOVE WITH KNIGHTS LIKE YOU DO.

SO WHERE ARE TERESA AND RODRIGO NOW?

Chapter 1

Changes and Challenges

I LIKE PLAYING "CONVENT." HURRY UP, "SISTER" JULIANA. PUT ON SOME PROPER CLOTHES. GOD IS WATCHING YOU.

BUT . . . "SISTER" . . . TERESA . . . THIS ROAD IS TOO DIFFICULT TO WALK.

PUFF

PANT

AND IT'S TOO HOT TODAY!

TSK TSK

AS A NUN, YOU CANNOT SAY "NO" TO A DIFFICULT ROAD. IF IT'S HARD, THE REWARD WILL BE BIGGER.

NO, NO, NO! I'M NOT PLAYING "LET'S MAKE BELIEVE WE'RE NUNS" ANYMORE. I'M TIRED!
HMPH!
HMPH!
BUT "SISTER" JULIANA, WE NEED TO COLLECT MORE HERBS.
YOU ALREADY COLLECTED A LOT. AND HOW DO YOU KNOW THAT THEY'RE MEDICINAL?
ALRIGHT, ALRIGHT . . .
ARE YOU ANGRY 'CAUSE I DON'T WANT TO PLAY ANYMORE?

NO, JULIANA. IT'S NOT THAT . . .
MAMÁ IS VERY SICK, AND THERE'S NOTHING I CAN DO TO HELP HER.
WHAT'S WRONG, TERESA?
EVEN A COUPLE OF WEEKS AGO I COULD STILL READ BOOKS TO HER. BUT SHE DOESN'T SEEM TO UNDERSTAND THEM ANYMORE.
I'M SO SCARED I WON'T HAVE MY MAMÁ ANYMORE.
TERESA . . .

ALTHOUGH NO LONGER A SMALL CHILD, TERESA WAS AFRAID OF HER MOTHER'S PALE FACE. KNOWING THAT HER MOTHER HAD PASSED AWAY, ALL TERESA COULD DO WAS CRY.

PLEASE, OPEN YOUR EYES . . .

SNIFF SNIFF

WHY DID GOD TAKE MAMÁ SO SOON?

SHE WAS SO NICE AND GENEROUS.

PLEASE ANSWER ME, MOTHER MARY . . .

HOW CAN I LIVE WITHOUT HER? I NEED A MOTHER.

WILL YOU BE MY MAMÁ NOW, MARY?

PLEASE HUG ME.

PLEASE COMFORT ME.

JUST LIKE MY MAMÁ USED TO DO.

YUCK! NO WAY! I'M NEVER GOING TO GET MARRIED TO HIM. HE'S FAT AND UGLY. I DON'T UNDERSTAND WHY MY PAPÁ CHOSE HIM FOR ME.

ARRGH

HEE, HEE, HEE

BUT, MY FRIEND, HE'S NICE AND HE SEEMS TO LIKE YOU A LOT.

EVEN SO . . .

I'D RATHER BE A MAIDEN AND KEEP DREAMING THAN MARRY SOMEONE LIKE HIM.

TERESA LOVED TO ATTEND PARTIES AND GO OUT WITH HER FRIENDS AS OFTEN AS SHE COULD. SHE THOUGHT MORE ABOUT CLOTHES AND GOSSIP THAN ABOUT GOD.

PAPÁ! DO I LOOK PRETTY? DOES THIS DRESS LOOK GOOD ON ME? I WISH I HAD A NICER DRESS, ESPECIALLY TODAY . . .

WHERE ARE YOU GOING, TERESA?

TERESA, I DON'T LIKE THAT DRESS. IT'S WAY TOO FLASHY.
YOUR MAMÁ ALWAYS LOOKED BEAUTIFUL EVEN THOUGH SHE WORE SIMPLE AND MODEST DRESSES.
SHE DID THAT BECAUSE SHE WAS OLD. ALL MY FRIENDS SAY I AM PRETTY. WHAT'S WRONG WITH YOU?
THEY THINK THAT I'M INTERESTING AND BEAUTIFUL. THEY LOVE ME, PAPÁ!
DON'T YOU WANT ME TO BE POPULAR? DON'T YOU WANT ME TO BE HAPPY?
NO, TERESA, THAT'S NOT THE POINT.
YOU'RE GETTING TOO SPOILED, TERESA. THIS IS NOT HOW YOU MAMÁ WOULD WANT YOU TO BE RAISED.

AND I DON'T THINK YOUR FRIENDS ARE ALL THAT NICE. THEY'RE NOT A GOOD INFLUENCE.
WHAT?! THEY'RE NICE PEOPLE, PAPÁ!
I'VE NOTICED YOU HAVEN'T BEEN PRAYING MUCH THESE DAYS, DEAR. PERHAPS IT'S BECAUSE OF THE FRIENDS YOU HAVE–
YES, I *HAVE* BEEN PRAYING! MAYBE YOU JUST DIDN'T SEE ME. I NEED TO LEAVE NOW AND MEET MY FRIENDS, ANYWAY. I DON'T WANT TO BE LATE.
WHERE ARE YOU GOING?
I'M GOING DANCING WITH MY FRIENDS.

OH, OK. BE CAREFUL AND DON'T BE LATE.

PAPÁ, IS TERESA GOING OUT AGAIN?

YES. I DON'T UNDERSTAND. SHE GOES OUT A LOT THESE DAYS.

MAYBE I JUST DON'T UNDERSTAND PEOPLE HER AGE.

22

PAPÁ, TERESA LOVES TO BE THE CENTER OF ATTENTION.
SHE WANTS ATTENTION AND SHE WANTS TO BE LOVED BY EVERYONE.
SHE TRIES TO LOOK BRAVE AND CONFIDENT BUT SHE'S LONELY.
SHE CHANGED A LOT AFTER MAMÁ DIED.
MARÍA, DO YOU THINK THAT TERESA IS GETTING OUT OF HAND, TOO?

LATER THAT NIGHT . . .

I NEED TO WALK IN VERY QUIETLY SO I DON'T WAKE UP MARÍA. JUST THE SLIGHTEST NOISE WILL WAKE HER SINCE SHE'S SUCH A LIGHT SLEEPER.

HELLO, TERESA. JUST GETTING HOME?

IT HAS BEEN DECIDED. WE'RE SENDING YOU TO STUDY WITH THE AUGUSTINIAN NUNS AT THE CONVENT OF HOLY MARY, OUR LADY OF GRACE.

I'VE HEARD THAT IT'S A GREAT SCHOOL. YOU'LL LIVE AND STUDY THERE.

IT WILL BE GOOD FOR YOU TO SPEND TIME WITH THE NUNS THERE. THEY'LL BE GOOD ROLE MODELS FOR YOU.

WHAT? WHY?! I HAVE A HOME! YOU CAN BE MY ROLE MODELS!

PAPÁ, I'M NOT THAT BAD!

TERESA, YOU'RE NOT *BAD*. BUT YOU DO HAVE TO CHANGE YOUR ATTITUDE.

BUT PAPÁ—

YOU'RE UNGRATEFUL FOR WHAT YOU HAVE AND HAVE BECOME QUITE SPOILED.

NO MORE ARGUING. YOU'RE LEAVING AS SOON AS IT CAN BE ARRANGED.

PLOP!

WHY ME? THIS IS SO UNFAIR!

I BET I'LL HAVE NO FRIENDS, NO PRETTY DRESSES, AND *NO* FUN WHILE I'M THERE!

WHY IS THIS HAPPENING TO ME, MOTHER MARY?!

Chapter 2

Learning and Listening

EVEN THOUGH I'VE BEEN AT THE SCHOOL* OF OUR LADY OF GRACE FOR A LITTLE WHILE, I'M STILL WORRIED THAT THE SISTERS AND THE OTHER GIRLS SEE ME AS PAPÁ DOES.

I MISS MY FRIENDS A LOT AND I'M A LITTLE BORED.

THAT GIRL . . .

DOES SHE LIKE IT HERE?

SHE *LOOKS* LIKE SHE'S HAPPY.

*IT WAS NOT UNCOMMON IN THE 1500S FOR GIRLS WHO WERE BOARDING AND STUDYING AT A CONVENT TO WEAR A UNIFORM AND VEIL, SIMILAR TO THE HABIT AND VEIL THAT THE RELIGIOUS SISTERS WORE.

MY NAME IS JUANA SUÁREZ.

THREE YEARS

I'M TERESA. I'VE BEEN HERE FOR ABOUT A MONTH. HOW LONG HAVE YOU BEEN HERE?

WOW! REALLY? DON'T YOU GET BORED HERE?

NOT REALLY. BEING IN A QUIET PLACE WHERE I CAN STUDY AND PRAY SUITS MY PERSONALITY.

EVER SINCE I WAS A LITTLE GIRL, I'VE WANTED TO BE A SISTER AND DO GOD'S WORK.

I'M SHY AND KEEP TO MYSELF. I REALLY DON'T LIKE BEING IN BIG CROWDS.

SO YOU WANT TO BE A NUN?

UH-HUH, THAT'S MY DREAM.

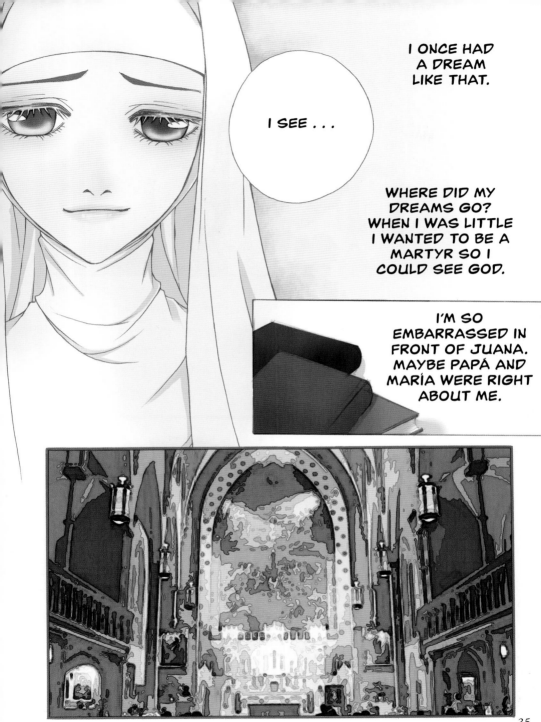

I ONCE HAD A DREAM LIKE THAT.

I SEE . . .

WHERE DID MY DREAMS GO? WHEN I WAS LITTLE I WANTED TO BE A MARTYR SO I COULD SEE GOD.

I'M SO EMBARRASSED IN FRONT OF JUANA. MAYBE PAPÁ AND MARÍA WERE RIGHT ABOUT ME.

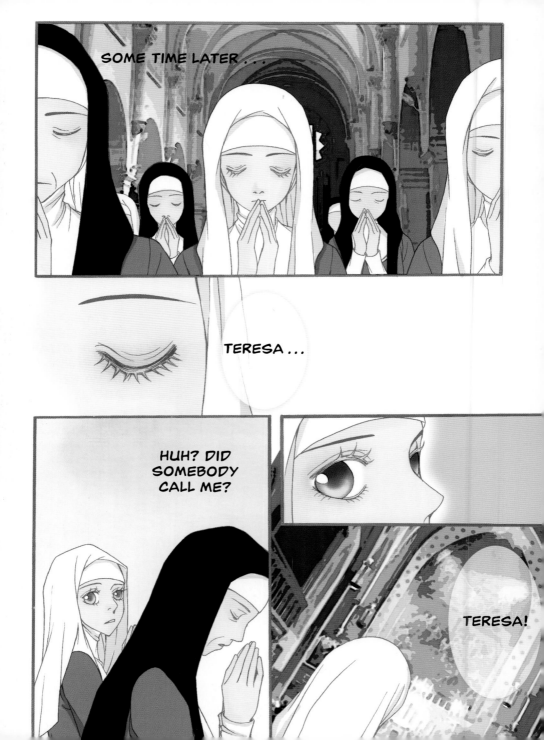

TERESA . . .
TERESA . . .

ARE YOU OK?

I WAS SO WORRIED. YOU FAINTED WHILE YOU WERE PRAYING. WHAT HAPPENED?

I DON'T KNOW. I HEARD A VOICE CALLING ME WHILE I WAS PRAYING . . .

A VOICE?

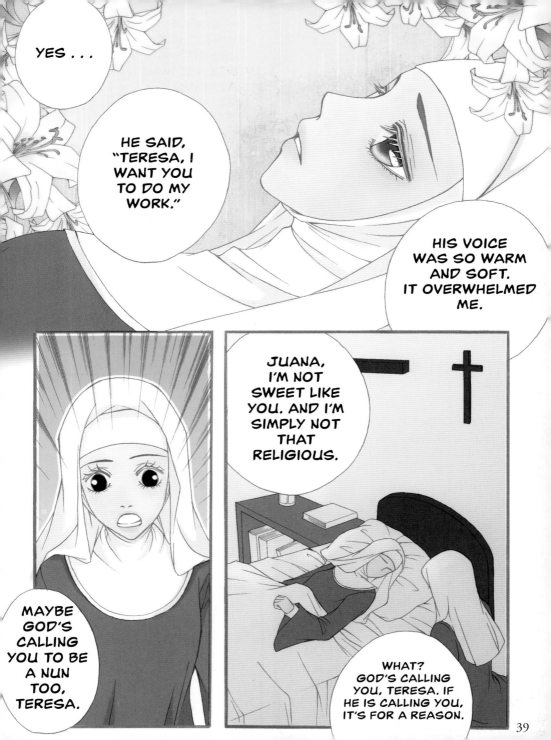

YES . . .

HE SAID, "TERESA, I WANT YOU TO DO MY WORK."

HIS VOICE WAS SO WARM AND SOFT. IT OVERWHELMED ME.

JUANA, I'M NOT SWEET LIKE YOU. AND I'M SIMPLY NOT THAT RELIGIOUS.

MAYBE GOD'S CALLING YOU TO BE A NUN TOO, TERESA.

WHAT? GOD'S CALLING YOU, TERESA. IF HE IS CALLING YOU, IT'S FOR A REASON.

TERESA PRAYED ABOUT WHAT GOD MIGHT BE ASKING HER TO DO WITH HER LIFE. SHE FELT AT PEACE WITH HER DECISION. THE TIME HAD COME TO TALK TO HER FATHER.

PAPÁ . . .

I HAVE SOMETHING TO TELL YOU.

WHAT IS IT? IT SOUNDS IMPORTANT.

YOU NEVER DO WHAT IS EXPECTED OF YOU!

I SENT YOU TO STUDY WITH THE NUNS BECAUSE I HOPED YOU WOULD BECOME MORE HARDWORKING AND HUMBLE. I DIDN'T SEND YOU THERE SO YOU COULD BECOME ONE OF THEM!

I WANT TO BE A CARMELITE NUN, PAPÁ. CAN'T YOU GIVE IT SOME THOUGHT?

WHY ARE YOU SO SET AGAINST THIS? WHY CAN'T I BE A NUN, PAPÁ?

WOULD YOU RATHER I IGNORE WHAT I FEEL GOD IS ASKING OF ME?

CARMELITE MONASTERY OF THE INCARNATION

DESPITE HIS MISGIVINGS, TERESA'S FATHER GAVE HER THE MONEY SHE NEEDED IN ORDER TO ENTER THE CARMELITES.

TIME JUST FLIES BY EVERY DAY HERE.

CONGRATULATIO TERESA! YOU'R GETTING USED LIFE IN OUR MONASTERY.

TRUE, BUT I'D BE EVEN HAPPIER IF THE SISTERS WHO MOCK ME WOULD STOP.

I DIDN'T REALIZE THERE WAS SO MUCH WORK TO DO IN KEEPING A PLACE CLEAN. IN THE PAST, I WOULDN'T DO THIS KIND OF WORK.

フゥゥ!

GASP

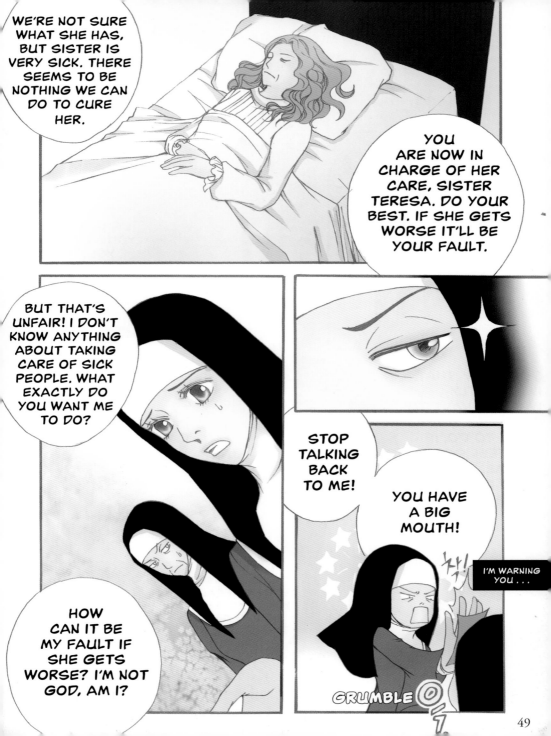

WITH THE EXCEPTION OF THE TIMES SHE WAS IN THE CHAPEL PRAYING, TERESA SPENT MOST OF HER TIME TAKING CARE OF THE SICK SISTER . . .

COME ON. JUST ONE MORE BITE.

SISTER TERESA, I'M SO SORRY THAT YOU HAD TO SKIP YOUR MEAL BECAUSE OF ME. I'M OK NOW. PLEASE GO EAT.

DON'T SAY THAT. I'M EXACTLY WHERE I WANT TO BE, DOING WHAT I WANT TO DO. IF YOU FEEL SORRY FOR ME, WELL, JUST GET BETTER SOON.

YEAH, BUT YOU'RE NOT SLEEPING WELL, SISTER TERESA, BECAUSE YOU'RE SO BUSY TAKING CARE OF ME EVEN AT NIGHT.

MAYBE SOON MY LIFE WILL BE OVER . . .

YOU MUST BE EXHAUSTED. YOU'VE BEEN TAKING CARE OF THIS SISTER ALL DAY AND NIGHT FOR QUITE A WHILE.
SISTER ISABEL IS SO MEAN MAKING YOU TAKE CARE OF HER. EVERYBODY ELSE AVOIDS IT BECAUSE CARING FOR HER IS SO DIFFICULT.
SHE DOESN'T SEEM TO BE GETTING ANY BETTER AND IF SHE DIES, YOU'LL FEEL GUILTY. WHY DID SISTER ISABEL MAKE YOU DO THIS?
BECAUSE SISTER ISABEL DOESN'T LIKE ME, JUANA.
I'M WORRIED ABOUT YOU, TERESA. YOU DON'T TAKE CARE OF YOUR OWN HEALTH BECAUSE YOU'RE ALWAYS TAKING CARE OF OUR SICK SISTER.
I'M FINE, JUANA. PLEASE DON'T WORRY ABOUT ME.

ACTUALLY, I'VE LEARNED A LOT ABOUT MYSELF WHILE TAKING CARE OF HER.

EVEN THOUGH SHE HAS SUCH TERRIBLE STOMACH PAIN, SISTER ALWAYS PUTS ME AND MY NEEDS BEFORE HER OWN.

WHEN I COMPARE MYSELF TO HER, I SEE HOW IMPATIENT AND IMMATURE I CAN BE.

I COULDN'T STAND IT IF SOMEBODY WERE TAKING CARE OF ME.

TERESA, YOU LOOK SO TIRED. PLEASE, GO AND REST NOW.

OH, TERESA, YOU HAVE A FEVER! ARE YOU FEELING OK?

53

ARE YOU AWAKE?
TERESA?
YOU'VE BEEN UNCONSCIOUS FOR A COUPLE OF DAYS. DO YOU REMEMBER ANYTHING?
I SENT A LETTER TO YOUR HOME. YOUR FATHER AND SISTER WILL BE HERE SOON TO GET YOU.
THEY'RE TAKING YOU TO A GREAT DOCTOR IN BECEDAS. I'LL BE GOING WITH YOU, TOO.
I'M JUST SO SLEEPY . . .

CLIP
CLOP

CLIP
CLOP

THE WHOLE WAY TO BECEDAS ALL I COULD THINK ABOUT WAS WHO WOULD BE TAKING CARE OF OUR SICK SISTER.

SISTER TERESA—ACCOMPANIED BY HER SISTER, FATHER, AND SISTER JUANA—GREW WEAKER DURING THE LONG TRIP TO BECEDAS.

WHY CAN'T I BE . . .

HEALTHY SO THE PEOPLE I LOVE DON'T HAVE TO WORRY?

FATHER, EVEN THOUGH I'M SICK I'VE BEEN ABLE TO DEEPEN MY PRAYER LIFE. MY BODY IS WEAKER BUT MY MIND IS CLEARER . . .

ALTHOUGH TERESA'S MIND AND WILL WERE STRONG, HER BODY WAS GETTING STEADILY WEAKER. REGARDLESS, SHE INSISTED ON GOING TO CONFESSION.

MY SELFISH DESIRES ARE DISAPPEARING. I WANT ONLY GOD.

IN THE PAST, I ALWAYS HUNGERED FOR ATTENTION. I ONLY CARED ABOUT WHAT I WANTED.

AM I CLOSER TO JESUS, FATHER?

THAT WAS AFTER MAMÁ DIED . . .

EVERYTHING HAS CHANGED. I NO LONGER FEEL EMPTY AND LONELY. JESUS HAS FILLED MY HEART WITH HIMSELF. AND I'M NOT CONTROLLED BY DESIRES ANY MORE.

YOU'RE NOT AS WEAK AS YOU THINK, SISTER TERESA.

SISTER TERESA, YOU KNOW YOU CAN SKIP CONFESSION SINCE YOU AREN'T FEELING WELL.

JESUS WILL UNDERSTAND IF YOU DON'T GO.

SISTER JUANA, CONFESSION MAKES ME FEEL AT PEACE.

I WONDER, WHAT'S GOING ON?

FATHER, I'M PROBABLY BEING RUDE, BUT CAN I ASK YOU SOMETHING?

WHAT IS IT?

WHO WAS THAT LADY YOU WERE WITH?

!!!

I'M SORRY, I'M PROBABLY BEING TOO NOSY. I'M JUST WORRIED . . .

I KNEW IT WAS WRONG . . . I DON'T DESERVE TO BE A PRIEST.

WERE YOU SEEING HER?

SLIPPING IN AND OUT OF CONSCIOUSNESS,

TERESA GREW WEAKER EACH DAY.

*IN SAINT TERESA'S TIME, THE SACRAMENT OF THE ANOINTING OF THE SICK—OFTEN CALLED EXTREME UNCTION—WAS ADMINISTERED ONLY WHEN A PERSON WAS DYING. TODAY, THIS SACRAMENT IS ADMINISTERED WHENEVER A PERSON HAS A SERIOUS ILLNESS OR IS FACING SURGERY.

I DON'T THINK SHE WILL EVER WAKE UP, PAPÁ.

WE SHOULD ASK A PRIEST TO ADMINISTER EXTREME UNCTION* NOW.

WHAT ARE YOU TALKING ABOUT, MARÍA? SHE IS *NOT* DYING.

BUT, PAPÁ, SHE'S BEEN UNCONSCIOUS FOR ALMOST TWO WEEKS. IT'S LIKE SHE'S DEAD.

SHE'S HARDLY BREATHING AND SHE LOOKS PALE AND LIFELESS.

69

TERESA, MY TERESA, IS *NOT* GOING TO DIE . . .

SO DON'T EVEN SUGGEST SUCH A THING.

OH LORD, PLEASE DON'T TAKE HER FROM US.

TERESA IS STILL YOUNG AND HAS SO MUCH LEFT TO DO.

YOU MUST BE TIRED, SISTER JUANA.
NO, NOT AT ALL. SITTING HERE AND PRAYING QUIETLY HELPS ME.
I FEAR TERESA WILL NOT RECOVER. SHE'S HARDLY MOVING AT ALL NOW.
SISTER, YOU PRAY FOR HER EVERY DAY WITHOUT MUCH REST. IF YOU KEEP THIS UP, I WORRY YOU'LL GET SICK TOO.

I WAS ALIVE.

AFTER A SHORT TIME OF RECOVERY TERESA WANTED TO GET BACK TO THE MONASTERY OF THE INCARNATION.

ARE YOU SURE YOU'RE OK? YOU DON'T NEED TO RUSH BACK TO THE MONASTERY. WHY DON'T YOU REST SOME MORE?

SISTER TERESA!

I'LL BE JUST FINE. SISTER JUANA WILL BE WITH ME.

OH, FATHER!

DON'T WORRY ABOUT SISTER TERESA, MARÍA. I PROMISE TO TAKE GOOD CARE OF HER.

CAN YOU STAY HERE IN BECEDAS?

FATHER, YOU KNOW THAT WE HAVE BOTH GIVEN OUR LIVES TO GOD. I CAN'T AND WON'T STAY HERE. I MUST GO BACK.

UH-UH

IF YOU STAY, I'D HELP YOU AND YOU COULD HELP ME. WE WOULD BOTH GROW CLOSER TO GOD.

I'VE BEEN ABLE TO STAY AWAY FROM MY MISTRESS BECAUSE OF YOUR ADVICE AND SUPPORT. CAN'T YOU PLEASE STAY AND HELP ME LIVE MY VOCATION AS A PRIEST?

도리

도리 NO

LOVING AND WORSHIPPING JESUS IN YOUR HEART IS THE BEST WAY TO FIGHT ALL THE TEMPTATIONS YOU EXPERIENCE, FATHER.

BY NOT GIVING IN TO THE TEMPTATIONS YOU WILL HAVE TRUE FREEDOM AS WELL AS TRUE HAPPINESS THAT CAN ONLY COME FROM GOD.

I AM LEAVING FOR THE MONASTERY, FATHER.

AND I LOOK FORWARD TO THE LIFE THAT IS AWAITING ME THERE.

TERESA RETURNED TO ÁVILA AND HER REPUTATION FOR GIVING GOOD AND HOLY ADVICE BECAME WELL KNOWN. PEOPLE WOULD OFTEN COME TO THE CONVENT ASKING TO SPEAK WITH HER.
THANK YOU SO MUCH, SISTER TERESA.
AFTER HAVING SPOKEN TO YOU I FEEL SO MUCH BETTER. I NO LONGER THINK ABOUT BAD THINGS AND I SLEEP LIKE A BABY.
I KNOW IT'S NOT MUCH, BUT WOULD YOU PLEASE ACCEPT THIS?
IT'S JUST A SMALL, INEXPENSIVE GIFT TO SHOW MY APPRECIATI FOR YOUR HELPFUL ADVIC PLEASE, TAKE IT.
OH NO, SEÑOR. I COULDN'T POSSIBLY ACCEPT THIS GRAND GIFT.

IF YOU REALLY WANT TO GIVE SOMETHING, YOU COULD BRING US SOME WILD FLOWERS THE NEXT TIME YOU VISIT.

THAT WOULD BE A GIFT WE COULD ALL ENJOY. WE COULD USE THEM IN CHAPEL.

SISTER TERESA!

DOÑA GUIOMAR DE ULLOA WANTS TO SPEAK TO YOU. SHE'S WAITING IN THE PARLOR.
I'LL GO THERE RIGHT AWAY.
YEESH! TERESA'S BECOME SO ARROGANT EVER SINCE ALL THOSE NOBLE MEN AND WOMEN BEGAN PAYING ATTENTION TO HER. I CAN'T STAND HER.
I BET SHE USES HER PRETTY FACE AND SWEET TALK TO BUY THEIR LOVE.
YEAH, YOU'RE PROBABLY RIGHT. HAHAHAHA . . .

WHAT ARE YOU TWO TALKING ABOUT? WATCH YOUR MOUTH AND THINK BEFORE YOU SPEAK.
SISTER TERESA IS FUNNY AND COMPASSIONATE. THAT'S WHY SHE'S SO POPULAR AND EVERYONE WANTS TO SPEAK TO HER.
SHE'S JUST BEING HERSELF; SHE'S VERY CHARMING.
WHAT'S WRONG WITH YOU? BECAUSE OF HER, PEOPLE ARE GROWING CLOSER TO GOD.
WHATEVER! PAY NO ATTENTION TO SISTER JUANA, SHE'S ANOTHER ONE OF TERESA'S FOLLOWERS!

THEY'RE SO MEAN! GOSSIPING BEHIND YOUR BACK, TERESA.
ALL THEY'RE GOOD FOR IS TALKING BAD ABOUT OTHERS. I'M SO ASHAMED OF THEM.
THEY'RE JUST JEALOUS OF YOU. NO MATTER WHAT THEY SAY, YOU'RE THE MOST POPULAR NUN HERE.
SISTER JUANA, I DON'T CARE WHAT THEY SAY ANYMORE. IT'S NOT THE FIRST TIME PEOPLE HAVE HATED ME WITHOUT GOOD REASON.
DON'T YOU THINK THAT'S UNFAIR? YOU DON'T DO ANYTHING WRONG AND STILL OTHERS BAD-MOUTH YOU.

JUST THE OTHER DAY I WAS SO UPSET WITH THEM THAT I ALMOST COULDN'T HOLD IN MY ANGER. BUT THEN I REALIZED IF I GET UPSET WITH THEM, THAT MEANS I LOSE AND THEY WIN.

PAT PAT

WOW! YOU ARE SO COOL, TERESA.

WHAT THEY SAY DOESN'T MATTER ANYMORE.

대인배! 이시기라!! YUP, YOU'RE THE BIGGER PERSON!

TERESA HAD FOUND PEACE OF HEART, BUT SOON HER WORLD WAS SHAKEN . . .

PAPÁ!
TERESA, THANK YOU FOR COMING SO QUICKLY.
WHAT HAPPENED? THIS SEEMS SO SUDDEN.
HE'S BEEN WORKING TOO MUCH. HE'S BEEN IN BED SINCE HE FAINTED A FEW DAYS AGO
HE SAID HE'S WAITING FOR YOU, TERESA.

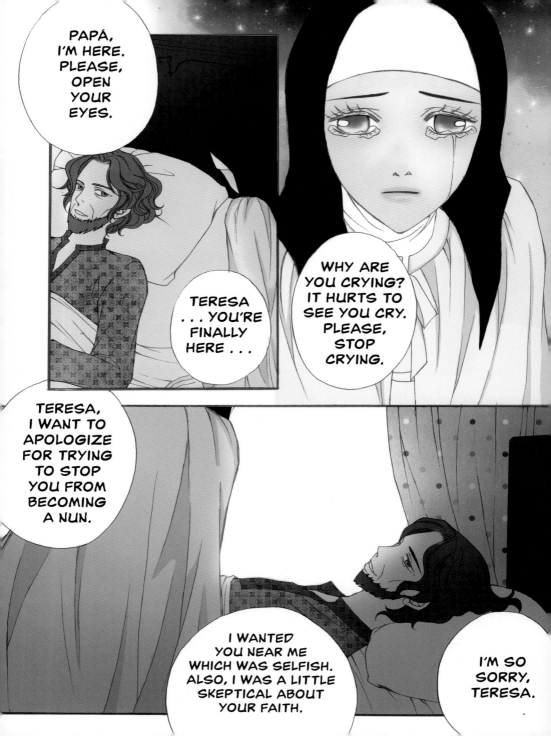

I ALWAYS MADE HIM WORRY ABOUT ME, AND I OFTEN HURT HIS FEELINGS.

HIS HEALTH MUST HAVE GOTTEN WORSE WHILE HE TOOK CARE OF ME IN BECEDAS.

MAYBE HIS DEATH IS MY FAULT.

THAT'S NOT TRUE. PAPÁ WAS A GOOD MAN AND GOD HAS CALLED HIM HOME. THINK HOW HAPPY PAPÁ IS RESTING IN THE LORD'S PEACE.

EVEN IF THIS IS GOD'S WILL . . .

I'M SAD BECAUSE I WON'T BE ABLE TO SEE PAPÁ AGAIN UNTIL WE ARE REUNITED IN HEAVEN.

STILL GRIEVING HER FATHER'S DEATH, SISTER TERESA RETURNED TO THE MONASTERY OF THE INCARNATION. IN PAIN SHE TURNED TO JESUS . . .

JESUS, YOUR MAJESTY,* I'M SO HURT.

* 'YOUR MAJESTY' IS ONE OF SAINT TERESA'S PREFERRED TERMS WHEN SPEAKING TO GOD.

PLEASE, HELP ME GET THROUGH THIS SADNESS.

TERESA!

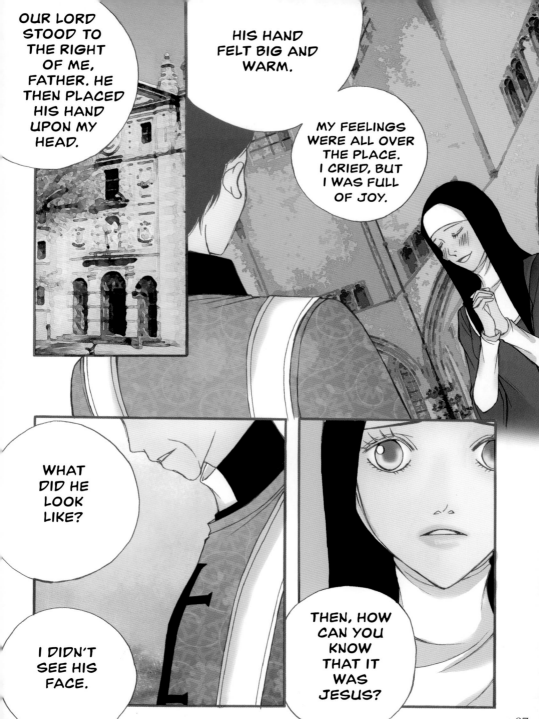

HAVE YOU HEARD ABOUT THE SCANDAL A SISTER FROM SEVILLE CAUSED?

절레

NUH-UH

SHE CLAIMED THAT SHE HAD A SPECIAL GIFT OF HEALING THE SICK. PEOPLE CAME FROM EVERYWHERE TO BE CURED.

SHE WAS KNOWN TO BE VERY PIOUS SO EVERYONE TRUSTED HER AND FOLLOWED HER.

BUT IT WAS ALL A LIE.

IT WAS LATER DISCOVERED THAT SINCE CHILDHOOD SHE HAD BEEN POSSESSED BY TWO DEMONS.

I'M SURE YOU KNOW WHY I'M TELLING YOU THIS STORY.

IT'S WISER IF YOU KEEP YOUR STORY ABOUT JESUS APPEARING TO YOU TO YOURSELF.

THE DEMONS CONTROLLED HER.

YOU DON'T WANT TO MISLEAD ANYONE.

FATHER, I WILL DO AS YOU RECOMMEND, AND STAY QUIET.

EVEN IF IT WASN'T THE DEVIL, MAYBE I WAS HALLUCINATING.

I'M NOT SURE ANYMORE THAT IT WAS JESUS.

DO YOU THINK SISTER TERESA'S CRAZY?

I THINK SHE'S ALWAYS TRYING TO BE THE CENTER OF ATTENTION. SHE'S NOTHING BUT A TROUBLESOME SCANDAL-MAKER IN OUR HOME.

YUP

YOU'RE RIGHT. SHE CAN'T BE GIFTED FROM GOD LIKE PEOPLE SAY; SHE'S NOT EVEN THAT GOOD OF A PERSON.

I'M PRETTY SURE SHE'S BEEN LYING.

WHAT DO I DO, JESUS?

NOBODY BELIEVES ME.

MAYBE IT WOULD BE BETTER IF THIS VISION WAS FROM THE DEVIL . . .

. . . THEN IT WOULDN'T BE SO PAINFUL.

LORD, WHY ARE YOU GIVING ME THIS PAIN?

I'M ONLY A WEAK AND ORDINARY WOMAN.

AND NOW PEOPLE HATE ME AND SAY HORRIBLE THINGS ABOUT ME.

FLUTTER
FLUTTER

WHAT DO
I DO?

THEN, RIGHT
IN FRONT OF
ME . . .

THERE
WAS AN
ANGEL.

OH . . .
THERE
ARE
WINGS . . .

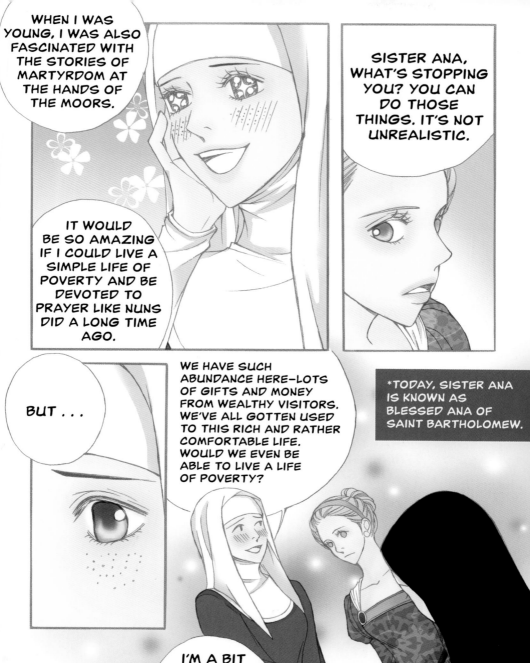

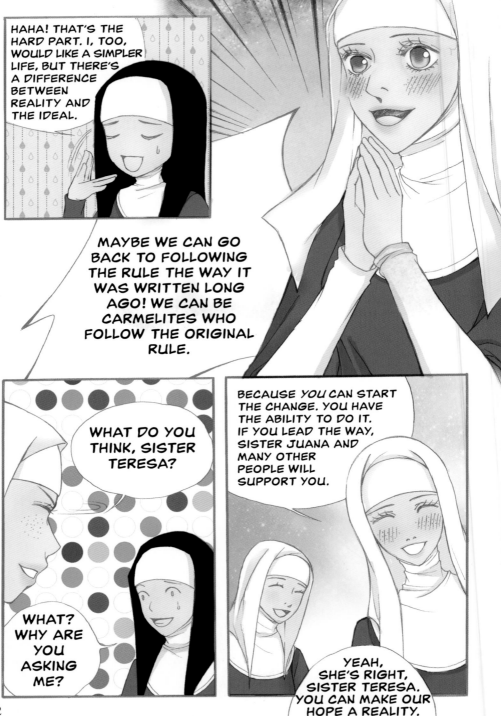

HAHA! THAT'S THE HARD PART. I, TOO, WOULD LIKE A SIMPLER LIFE, BUT THERE'S A DIFFERENCE BETWEEN REALITY AND THE IDEAL.

MAYBE WE CAN GO BACK TO FOLLOWING THE RULE THE WAY IT WAS WRITTEN LONG AGO! WE CAN BE CARMELITES WHO FOLLOW THE ORIGINAL RULE.

WHAT DO YOU THINK, SISTER TERESA?

WHAT? WHY ARE YOU ASKING ME?

BECAUSE *YOU* CAN START THE CHANGE. YOU HAVE THE ABILITY TO DO IT. IF YOU LEAD THE WAY, SISTER JUANA AND MANY OTHER PEOPLE WILL SUPPORT YOU.

YEAH, SHE'S RIGHT, SISTER TERESA. YOU CAN MAKE OUR HOPE A REALITY.

IT'S NOT THAT EASY, SISTERS. IT'S NOT A DECISION TO BE TAKEN LIGHTLY.
IN ADDITION, I'M JUST AN ORDINARY NUN. HOW CAN I?
YOU'RE NOT AN ORDINARY NUN, SISTER TERESA. YOU'RE SPECIAL.
DON'T LET THE FINANCIAL SIDE STOP YOU FROM STARTING A NEW MONASTERY. I'M PRETTY SURE I CAN GET SOME FRIENDS TO DONATE MONEY OR LAND.
WE CAN MAKE THIS HAPPEN TOGETHER, SISTER TERESA!

JESUS, DO *YOU* WANT ME TO START A NEW FOUNDATION?

YOU KNOW HOW MUCH I WANT TO LIVE A LIFE OF POVERTY, JUST LIKE THE MARTYRS DID, BUT . . .

I'M WEAK AND MY HEALTH IS NOT GOOD.

TERESA, MY DAUGHTER, I AM CALLING YOU TO DO THIS BECAUSE IT IS MY WILL TO HAVE AN ORDER OF CARMELITES WHO LIVE A MORE ASCETIC* LIFE.

YOU PROMISED TO OBEY AND TRUST ME.

*ASCETICISM IS THE PRACTICE OF SELF-DENIAL AS A SPIRITUAL DISCIPLINE.

YOUR MAJESTY, WHY ARE YOU GIVING ME SUCH AN IMPOSSIBLE TASK?

I WANT TO LIVE A LIFE OF POVERTY, LORD, AND THAT MAKES IT HARDER FOR ME TO COLLECT THE FUNDS WE WOULD NEED TO START.

WHAT DO YOU EXPECT FROM A PERSON LIKE ME?

TERESA, IF THIS TASK WERE IMPOSSIBLE, I WOULDN'T ASK YOU TO TAKE IT ON.

TRUST ME, MY DAUGHTER. YOU ARE STRONG, BRAVE, AND BOLD ENOUGH TO DO THIS.

YOU ARE NOT ALONE; I AM WITH YOU EVERY STEP OF THE WAY. DO NOT HESITATE TO ASK ME FOR HELP.

AFTER MUCH PRAYER SISTER TERESA ACCEPTED GOD'S INVITATION TO LIVE THE CARMELITE RULE IN A DIFFERENT WAY. SOME NUNS WOULD STAY WITH THE CARMELITES AND CONTINUE THEIR LIFE AS IT HAD BEEN. OTHERS WOULD JOIN TERESA AND THE CARMELITES OF THE REFORM.

WHAT?! ARE YOU OUT OF YOUR MIND, SISTER TERESA?! A *REFORMED* CARMELITE ORDER? FOLLOWING THE ORIGINAL PRIMITIVE RULE?
YES, FATHER. THIS IS WHAT GOD IS ASKING ME TO DO . . .
TO REFORM CARMEL TO A MORE STRICT OBSERVANCE OF THE VOW OF POVERTY.
DO YOU CARE NOTHING ABOUT MY PREVIOUS WARNING? I TOLD YOU TO BE CAREFUL. WHY ARE YOU CHOOSING A MORE DIFFICULT PATH?
THE OTHER SISTERS ALREADY HATE YOU. YOU'LL BE OSTRACIZED EVEN MORE.

REGARDLESS OF HOW OTHERS FEEL ABOUT ME, REGARDLESS OF THE DIFFICULTY OF THE PATH, I CHOOSE TO OBEY GOD. I WILL NOT GO AGAINST HIS WILL FOR ME.

THAT PLAN IS NOT REALISTIC. YOU *STILL* THINK THOSE VISIONS YOU HAD WERE REAL? THEY WERE PROBABLY EVIL HALLUCINATIONS!

SLAM

쿵!

HE'S DOUBTING YOU, JESUS. PLEASE BE MERCIFUL AND FORGIVE HIM.

ARRGH

ARE YOU KIDDING ME? YOU'RE GOING TO BE THE LAUGHING STOCK OF ÁVILA!

DON'T WORRY, FATHER. GOD IS IN CHARGE OF THIS PLAN.

JESUS, AS LONG AS YOU ARE WITH ME, I WILL BE ABLE TO COMPLETE YOUR WORK.

AS TERESA PRAYED FOR GUIDANCE AND WAITED TO BEGIN THE REFORM, SHE WAS ABLE TO FIND SUPPORT FROM FRIENDS AND BENEFACTORS.

WHEN OTHERS WERE POINTING THEIR FINGERS AND SAYING I COULDN'T DO ANYTHING BECAUSE I HAD NO COMMON SENSE . . .

YOU BELIEVED IN ME.

WHEN I WAS IN PAIN YOU TOLD ME, "BE BRAVE, CHEER UP. . . .

GOD ALWAYS SHOWS HIS POWER THROUGH THE WEAK."

IN AUGUST OF 1562 THE FOUNDATION OF THE MONASTERY OF ST. JOSEPH BEGAN. FOUR NOVICES ENTERED: SISTER ANTONIA, SISTER MARÍA, SISTER URSULA, AND SISTER MARÍA OF ÁVILA. TWO SISTERS FROM THE INCARNATION, SISTER INÉS AND SISTER ANA, ALSO JOINED TERESA; OTHERS WOULD FOLLOW. WITH THE REFORM TERESA TOOK THE NAME TERESA OF JESUS.

FINALLY, WE HAVE OUR OWN CONVENT. IT'S TINY BUT COZY. THIS IS SO EXCITING, SISTER TERESA!

DON'T GET TOO EXCITED. DON'T FORGET WE STILL HAVE TONS OF WORK TO DO.

LET'S START CLEANING, SISTERS. THIS PLACE IS A MESS.

YES, MADRE!*

네~~

*MADRE MEANS 'MOTHER' IN SPANISH AND IS A TERM OF RESPECT USED FOR RELIGIOUS SISTERS.

ALTHOUGH EXCITED ABOUT THE NEW MONASTERY TERESA WAS PLAGUED BY QUESTIONS. SHE WORRIED THAT SHE WAS SOMEHOW NOT DOING GOD'S WILL.

AM I RIGHT IN DOING THIS?

WHAT IF WE CAN'T GET ENOUGH FOOD? WILL I BE HAPPY LIVING WITH SO LITTLE?

DO YOU REMEMBER WHEN YOUR MAMÁ PASSED AWAY . . . YOU ASKED ME TO BE YOUR MOTHER AND I ACCEPTED . . .

Chapter 4

Facing
the Crisis

MADRE, A LETTER CAME FOR YOU.

WHO'S IT FROM?

A LETTER? THANK YOU, SISTER ANA, MAY I HAVE IT?

IT'S FROM DON RAFAEL MEJÍA IN DURUELO. HE'S OFFERING TO DONATE ONE OF HIS FARMHOUSE FOR A NEW FOUNDATION.

WOW

WE'RE RECEIVING A LOT OF HELP FROM PEOPLE EVERYWHERE. ISN'T THAT GREAT, MADRE?

YES, SISTER ANA, BUT WE ALSO HAVE ENEMIES. THERE ARE THOSE WHO ARE TRYING TO STOP US. EVERYTHING IS A TWO-SIDED COIN.

I HEARD YOU ARE GOING TO MEDINA. COULD I ACCOMPANY YOU, PLEASE?

YES!

이스트!

SURE! LET'S MAKE THIS HAPPEN.

MEDINA DEL CAMPO, SPAIN

135

I ASKED YOU TO COME HERE BECAUSE I'VE HEARD ABOUT YOU AND I'M REALLY INTERESTED IN THE REFORMATION OF THE CARMELITE ORDER YOU HAVE STARTED.
I WOULD LIKE YOU TO HELP REFORM THE FRIARY AS WELL.
OH, FRIAR ANTONIO! I'M HAPPY TO HAVE THE OPPORTUNITY TO SERVE. THERE ARE MANY PEOPLE WHO SUPPORT US.
YOU'RE BEING HUMBLE, MADRE. NEWS HAS REACHED US ABOUT HOW YOU HAVE SUCCESSFULLY OPENED OTHER REFORMED CONVENTS.
IS THAT SO? I'M EMBARRASSED. BUT THOSE WERE ALL FOR NUNS . . .

THERE ARE SOME OF US MEN WHO ALSO WANT THE KIND OF LIFE YOU'RE LIVING. THERE IS ANOTHER FRIAR HERE WHO IS UNHAPPY WITH THE LAX LIFE WE'RE LIVING. MAY I INTRODUCE YOU TO HIM?

FRIAR JOHN WAS INDEED MOST UNHAPPY WITH THE WAY THE CARMELITE FRIARS LIVED. HE LONGED FOR A MUCH STRICTER OBSERVANCE OF THE RULE AND WAS CONSIDERING LEAVING THE CARMELITES AND ENTERING ANOTHER ORDER CALLED THE CARTHUSIANS.

HELLO, FRIAR JOHN.*

*FRIAR JOHN WAS 25 YEARS OLD AND SISTER TERESA WAS 52 YEARS OLD. WHEN HE JOINED THE REFORM HE TOOK THE NAME FRIAR JOHN OF THE CROSS. HE IS ALSO A SAINT.

DO I KNOW YOU? HAVE WE MET BEFORE?

MY NAME IS TERESA AND I'M FROM THE MONASTERY OF ST. JOSEPH IN ÁVILA. FRIAR ANTONIO SPOKE TO ME ABOUT YOU.

WHAT DID HE SAY?

THAT YOU'RE VERY INTELLIGENT, VERY PIOUS, A BIT ON THE QUIET SIDE, AND AN ALL-AROUND GOOD PERSON.

SO? WHY DID YOU WANT TO MEET ME?

HMM. HE SEEMS RATHER DISTANT AND INFLEXIBLE . . .

SOMEONE IN DURUELO DONATED A FARMHOUSE FOR US TO USE FOR A NEW MONASTERY.

WE'RE REFORMING CARMELITE MONASTERIES TO A MORE STRICT OBSERVANCE OF THE PRIMITIVE RULE.

ALTHOUGH IT'S TINY AND OLD, IT WILL SUIT OUR PURPOSES FOR A SIMPLE WAY OF LOVING AND SERVING GOD.

WHAT DO YOU SAY, FRIAR JOHN?

WOULD YOU LIKE TO JOIN US?

AT FIRST THEY WERE ZEALOUS AND ENERGETIC.

IN MY SHORT TIME AS A CARMELITE I HAVE COME TO KNOW A LOT OF FRIARS.

BUT AS TIME WENT BY, THEY BECAME LAZY AND FORGOT WHY THEY WANTED TO GIVE THEIR LIVES TO GOD.

PEOPLE MAKE FUN OF ME. THEY CALL ME HEADSTRONG AND STUPID AND A FREAK. BUT I KNOW HOW GOD IS CALLING ME TO LIVE, WHICH IS WHY I CHOOSE TO HIDE AWAY AND LIVE VERY SIMPLY.

HOW CAN YOU BE SO SURE THAT I WILL BE LIKE THE OTHERS YOU MENTIONED?

IF YOU ARE A FREAK BECAUSE YOU WANT TO LIVE SIMPLY, THEN SO AM I.
IF I WEREN'T A FREAK, I WOULDN'T WORK SO HARD AGAINST SO MUCH ADVERSITY FOR THIS IDEAL.
I PROMISE I'LL NEVER TURN MY BACK ON THIS REFORMED RULE. I'LL NEVER GIVE UP ON WHAT GOD IS ASKING ME TO DO AND LIVE.
I GIVE YOU MY WORD, FRIAR JOHN.
IMAGINE HOW AMAZING IT WOULD BE IF WE TWO FREAKS COULD GIVE OURSELVES COMPLETELY TO GOD'S WILL.

AFTER SIX MONTHS A SMALL COMMUNITY OF FRIARS OF THE REFORM MOVED INTO THEIR NEW HOME IN DURUELO. THE COMMUNITY WAS MADE UP OF THREE FRIARS: FRIAR ANTONIO OF JESUS, FRIAR JOHN OF THE CROSS, AND FRIAR JOSEPH OF CHRIST.

PRAISE GOD! THE MALE BRANCH OF THE CARMELITES WILL ALSO BENEFIT FROM THE REFORM MOVEMENT. GOOD WORK, MADRE TERESA!

I DIDN'T DO ANYTHING. I THANK GOD FOR FRIAR JOHN'S STRONG SUPPORT AND SURE DEDICATION TO A SIMPLE LIFE.

143

WHAT?

YOU WANT ME TO BE PRIORESS* AT THE MONASTERY OF THE INCARNATION? BUT THEY DON'T FOLLOW THE REFORM. IT DOESN'T MAKE SENSE.

WHY *ME*? I'M SURE THERE ARE SISTERS WHO ARE ALREADY THERE WHO ARE BETTER SUITED FOR THE JOB.

SISTER TERESA, IN MY OPINION, YOU ARE THE BEST PERSON.

THE SISTERS HAVE GROWN LAZY. THEY NEED SOMEONE WHO WILL GUIDE THEM WITH LOVE AND A FIRM HAND. THERE IS NO ONE ELSE BUT YOU.

*THE PRIORESS IS THE NUN WHO IS IN CHARGE OF A RELIGIOUS HOUSE OR MONASTERY.

THESE SISTERS WILL NOT FOLLOW YOUR REFORM BUT THEY DO NEED TO LIVE THEIR VOWS.

146

EVEN THOUGH YOU'RE WORRIED ABOUT THE MONASTERIES OF THE REFORMED RULE IF YOU BECOME PRIORESS AT THE MONASTERY OF THE INCARNATION...

MEANWHILE AT THE MONASTERY OF THE INCARNATION . . .

I CAN'T UNDERSTAND HOW THAT WOMAN CAN BE *OUR* PRIORESS.

. . . DO NOT WORRY. WITH MY HELP, YOU WILL BE ABLE TO DO BOTH.

I AM HERE TO SUPPORT YOU, SISTERS.

I HOPE YOU'LL SUPPORT ME AS WELL, EVEN IF YOU DON'T LIKE ME.

WOO-HOO! THAT WENT SO WELL! THEY AGREED WITH EVERYTHING YOU SAID—THEY WERE SPEECHLESS!

랄랄라~

HMM HMM

SISTER ANA! DON'T SAY THAT!

WHY NOT? IF YOU ONLY KNEW WHAT THEY WERE SAYING BEHIND YOUR BACK! EVERYONE WAS MAKING FUN OF YOU!
I THINK YOU'RE TOO NICE TO THE OTHER SISTERS, MADRE. THEY'VE ALWAYS ANSWERED YOUR KINDNESS WITH BITTERNESS.
PLEASE DON'T SAY THAT, SISTER ANA. HOW ELSE SHOULD I ACT? A PRIORESS NEEDS TO SERVE OTHERS AND NOT USE HER POWER TO CONTROL THEM.
BUT IT'S UNFAIR. YOU COULD'VE BEEN BOSSIER. DON'T YOU AGREE SISTER JUANA?
BLUSH
치이!...
YOU WOULDN'T WANT AN UNCHARITABLE AND BOSSY PRIORESS, RIGHT?
SISTER ANA, SISTER JUANA, THAT IS NOT GOD'S WAY.

TERESA CARRIED OUT HER RESPONSIBILITIES AS PRIORESS WITH GREAT LOVE FOR THE SISTERS. THE SISTERS GREW TO RESPECT TERESA AND ALTHOUGH THEY DID NOT JOIN HER REFORM THEY RETURNED TO A BETTER OBSERVANCE OF THEIR RULE. WHILE SHE WAS PRIORESS SHE WAS STILL ABLE TO OPEN MORE MONASTERIES OF THE REFORM. SHE SERVED AS PRIORESS AT THE MONASTERY OF THE INCARNATION FROM 1571 UNTIL 1574 WHEN SHE WAS ALLOWED TO RETURN TO LIVE WITH OTHER CARMELITE SISTERS OF THE REFORM.

I HEARD THAT WHILE YOU WERE PRIORESS OF THE INCARNATION, YOU MANAGED TO CONTINUE YOUR WORK OF REFORM.

MADRE, MAY GOD CONTINUE TO GIVE YOU THE ENERGY YOU NEED!

HAHAHA! I ENVY YOUR UNTIRING ENERGY.

I ONLY DID WHAT GOD ASKED ME TO DO. I'M NOT THE KIND OF PERSON WHO STARTS THINGS AND NEVER FINISHES THEM.

HAHA . . . JUST LIKE PEOPLE SAID! YOU'RE SO STRAIGHTFORWARD!

155

MADRE, JESUS TOLD HIS DISCIPLES HE DIDN'T HAVE A PLACE TO LAY HIS HEAD.

IN TIME, TERESA RETURNED TO THE MONASTERY OF SAINT JOSEPH IN ÁVILA . . .

DID YOU MEET FRIAR GRACIÁN, MADRE?

ANY OBSTACLE IS EASY WHEN COMPARED WITH HIS.

YES, SISTER ANA. HE'S VERY NICE AND KIND.

HE ALSO FAITHFULLY SUPPORTS OUR REFORMS OF THE ORDER.

SISTER ANA, YOU ARE DEVELOPING A BAD HABIT OF SPREADING RUMORS. HOW CAN YOU ASK ME SUCH A QUESTION?
BOTH FRIAR JOHN AND FRIAR GRACIÁN ARE LIKE MY SONS. I WON'T LET YOU TALK THAT WAY ABOUT THEM.
I HEARD FRIAR GRACIÁN'S NICKNAME IS SAINT PAUL BECAUSE HE LOOKS LIKE SAINT PAUL.
SISTER ANA, PLEASE REMEMBER YOUR VOWS.
I RESPECT FRIAR GRACIÁN. HE'S SMART AND GENEROUS EVEN THOUGH HE'S STILL SO YOUNG.
HE COULD BE THE ONE GOD WILL USE TO SPREAD THE REFORMS OF THE CARMELITE ORDER LONG AFTER I AM GONE.

NOT EVERYONE WAS IN FAVOR OF THE REFORM. SOME MEMBERS OF THE MALE CARMELITES WHO DID NOT FOLLOW THE REFORM WANTED TO STOP SISTER TERESA AND THE FRIARS . . .

타! SLAM

WHAT ARE YOU GOING TO DO ABOUT SISTER TERESA? SHE'S RUINING THE ORDER BY TRYING TO CHANGE OUR WAY OF LIFE!

SHE PROBABLY THINKS WE CARE ONLY ABOUT MONEY, THAT WE'RE VAIN AND LAZY. SHE'S EVEN GOTTEN SOME OF OUR FRIARS TO JOIN HER REFORM. DO YOU STILL THINK WE CAN JUST IGNORE WHAT SHE'S TRYING TO DO?

NO WAY! WE CAN'T IGNORE HER MEDDLING ANY MORE.

HOW DARE SHE TRY TO REFORM US! WHO DOES SHE THINK SHE IS?! DOES SHE THINK SHE'S BETTER THAN US?

WE CAN'T JUST SIT AROUND AND SEE WHAT HAPPENS. WE NEED TO DO SOMETHING ABOUT HER REFORM ATTEMPTS.

WE'LL SHOW THE REST OF THEM HOW TO HANDLE SOMEONE LIKE SISTER TERESA.

STOMP STOMP

STOMP STOMP

WHERE'S SISTER TERESA?

SMASH

WHO ARE YOU? WHAT ARE YOU DOING?!

ARE *YOU* SISTER TERESA?

I HAVE AN ORDER FROM THE PRIOR GENERAL OF THE CARMELITES. YOU MUST LEAVE AT ONCE. YOU'D BETTER FOLLOW ME.

YES. WHY ARE YOU HERE?

THE PERSECUTION OF THE REFORM MOVEMENT CONTINUED. THEIR NEXT TARGET WAS FRIAR JOHN OF THE CROSS.

PLEASE STOP CRYING, SISTER ANA.
I DON'T UNDERSTAND. WHY ARE THEY DOING THIS, MADRE?
SNIFF SOB SNIFF SOB
I DON'T KNOW. I'M JUST SO WORRIED THAT FRIAR JOHN IS BEING TERRIBLY MISTREATED.
MADRE, IS THERE ANYTHING YOU CAN DO?
I DON'T KNOW. AND NOW THEY'RE HOLDING FRIAR GRACIÁN, TOO.

WHEN FRIAR GRACIÁN HEARD THAT FRIAR JOHN OF THE CROSS WAS TAKEN . . .

HE CALLED A MEETING ABOUT SEPARATING THE OBSERVANT CARMELITE ORDER AND THE REFORMED ORDER.

OH OUR POOR FRIARS! ACTING WITHOUT THE APPROVAL OF THE OFFICIAL VICAR GENERAL COULD MAKE THINGS WORSE. MAY GOD PROTECT THEM BOTH.

THIS IS ALL MY FAULT. IF I HADN'T STARTED THE REFORM, NONE OF THIS WOULD BE HAPPENING TO THEM. BOTH FRIAR JOHN AND FRIAR GRACIÁN ARE SO GOOD. THEY DON'T DESERVE THIS.

I KNEW THAT HAVING SISTER TERESA AROUND WAS A MISTAKE. I TOLD YOU THAT YOU NEEDED TO HAVE SOMEONE ELSE IN CHARGE.

WHY WOULD WE NEED SOMEONE ELSE? WE ALREADY HAVE MADRE TERESA.

SISTER TERESA DOESN'T DESERVE THAT HONOR. SHE LOOKS DOWN ON ALL OF YOU AND SOME SAY SHE HAD AFFAIRS WITH TWO PRIESTS.

DON'T LISTEN TO THOSE RUMORS. SHE'S COMPLETELY INNOCENT.

169

SISTER TERESA SHOULD NO LONGER BE IN CHARGE! SHALL I CHOOSE SOMEONE NEW FOR YOU RIGHT NOW?

IF YOU CAN.

HOW DARE YOU, SISTER! DO YOU EVEN KNOW WHO I AM?!

IT DOESN'T MATTER WHO YOU ARE. WE ALREADY HAVE A SUPERIOR— MADRE TERESA DE JESÚS.

WE WILL WAIT FOR HER TO RETURN FROM HER TRAVELS. WE DON'T NEED OR WANT A NEW SUPERIOR.

TERESA! TAKE COURAGE, MY DAUGHTER. YOU MUST EAT.
I DON'T WANT TO EAT ANYTHING. I AM WORRIED FOR MY TWO SONS WHO ARE BEING MISTREATED.
TERESA, IF YOU LOVE ME, EAT THIS.
WILL YOU NOT DO AS I ASK, MY DAUGHTER? TAKE AND EAT.
JESUS BROKE SOME BREAD AND THEN FED TERESA. SHE OBEDIENTLY ATE WHAT HE GAVE HER.

SQUIRE! WHAT IS THE SITUATION ABOUT WHICH MADRE TERESA DE JESÚS WROTE IN THIS LETTER? IS THERE SOMETHING GOING ON IN MY KINGDOM WITHOUT MY APPROVAL?
SISTER TERESA'S LETTER FINALLY REACHED THE KING IN MADRID. IN KING PHILIP II SHE HAD AN ALLY FOR THE REFORM OF THE CARMELITE RULE.
YOUR MAJESTY THE TABLISHED CARMELITES HAVE BEEN HARSHLY ERSECUTING THOSE OF THE REFORM. THEY'VE EVEN CAPTURED FRIAR JOHN OF THE CROSS TO FORCE HIM TO STOP THE REFORM.
YOUR HIGHNESS, EVEN YOUR FRIEND, FRIAR GRACIÁN, HAS BEEN DETAINED AND HELD AGAINST HIS WILL IN A MONASTERY.
WHAT? HOW CAN THIS BE?!
WHY AM I JUST HEARING ABOUT THIS NOW?

THOSE MEN AREN'T SINNERS. PLEASE, IN YOUR KINDNESS HELP THE CARMELITES OF THE REFORM, YOUR MAJESTY.

I TRUST MADRE TERESA AND THE TWO FRIARS. I BELIEVE THEY ARE TRYING TO DO GOD'S WILL.

CALL THE VICAR GENERAL AND TELL HIM I WANT THESE MEN RELEASED. ALSO, TELL HIM I WANT A FULL REPORT OF WHAT HAPPENED. I DON'T WANT THIS TO EVER HAPPEN AGAIN!

AFTER MORE THAN EIGHT
HEART-WRENCHING MONTHS
OF WAITING AND WORRYING
ABOUT HER SONS . . .

MADRE!

JESUS HAS SENT GOOD PEOPLE . . .

TO PROTECT MY TWO SONS.

HE LISTENED TO MY PRAYERS AND STAYED CLOSE TO ME.

MY TEARS ARE FULL OF JOY AND THANKSGIVING FOR EVERYTHING GOD HAS DONE FOR ME.

*LITERALLY, 'CALCED' MEANS WITH SHOES AND 'DISCALCED' MEANS WITHOUT SHOES. DISCALCED CARMELITES TRADITIONALLY WEAR SANDALS INSTEAD OF SHOES.

IN 1580, WITH POPE GREGORY XIII'S APPROVAL, THE CARMELITES WERE ALLOWED TO SEPARATE INTO TWO DISTINCT ORDERS. ONE IS KNOWN AS THE MITIGATED OR CALCED CARMELITES, THE OTHER IS NOW KNOWN AS THE DISCALCED CARMELITES—THE REFORMED ORDER SISTER TERESA STARTED.*

AFTER ALL THE SUFFERING AND OBSTACLES, WE FINALLY HAVE APPROVAL TO LIVE ACCORDING TO THE PRIMITIVE RULE WITHOUT FEAR AND CAN CONTINUE OPENING MONASTERIES OF THE REFORM.

GOD'S WILL FOR OUR ORDER HAS FINALLY BEEN DONE. IT MAY HAVE TAKEN MANY YEARS, BUT PRAISE GOD FOR SEEING US THROUGH THIS TIME.

Chapter5

Daughter of the Church

FRIAR, ISN'T IT INCONVENIENT TO HAVE THE DOORS HERE? AND THAT DINING ROOM IS WAY TOO SMALL.

SISTER TERESA CONTINUED TO TRAVEL THROUGHOUT SPAIN VISITING FOUNDATIONS AND OPENING NEW HOUSES. TERESA'S HEALTH HAD NEVER BEEN EXCELLENT AND A TRIP TO ALBA DE TORMES IN 1582 TOOK A TOLL ON HER.

MADRE, THE SIMPLICITY OF THE HOUSE IS FINE FOR US. YOU'LL SEE THAT SOON.

SISTER TERESA!

WHY AREN'T YOU RESTING?! YOU KNOW YOU'RE NOT WELL.

UH-OH! SHE CAUGHT ME.

이크...
들켰다...

I SHOULD NEVER HAVE BROUGHT YOU HER. DESPITE YOUR INSISTENCE, I SHOULDN'T HAVE LET YOU COME. HOW WILL YOU EVER GE BETTER?

182

WHAT?! DID YOU SAY MADRE TERESA PASSED OUT?

YES, SISTER JUANA. SISTER ANA IS WITH HER AND SHE SAYS THAT MADRE IS IN BED.

NOT YET . . .

PLEASE, NOT YET, JESUS!

SISTER JUANA RUSHED TO ALBA DE TORMES.

185

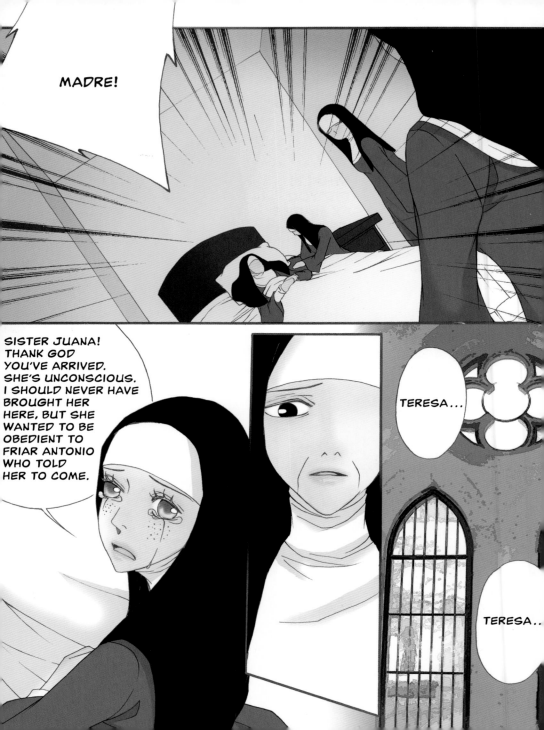

MY DEAR JUANA, YOU ALWAYS MANAGE TO WAKE ME UP FROM THE DEEPEST SLEEP.

PLEASE DON'T CRY.

LISTEN CLOSELY MY DAUGHTERS— LOVE GOD BY FOLLOWING THE RULE HE HAS GIVEN US AND LIVE A SIMPLE LIFE OF POVERTY, DEVOTED TO PRAYER.

AND I BEG YOU, IF I HAVE EVER HURT YOUR FEELINGS, PLEASE FORGIVE ME.

MADRE, BE AT PEACE. YOU'VE NEVER HURT US. WE ALL TRUST YOU AND LOVE YOU.

MY SOUL IS
FULL OF JOY
BECAUSE NOW
I CAN BE
WITH YOU
COMPLETELY.

"CREATE IN ME A CLEAN HEART, O GOD, AND PUT A NEW AND RIGHT SPIRIT WITHIN ME.

THE SACRIFICE ACCEPTABLE
TO GOD IS A BROKEN SPIRIT;
A BROKEN AND CONTRITE
HEART, O GOD, YOU WILL NOT
DESPISE."

—PSALM 51: 10, 17

Let nothing disturb you
Let nothing frighten you.
All things are passing.
God alone never changes
Patience gains all things.
If you have God you will
Want for nothing.
God alone suffices.

—Found in Saint Teresa of Avila's notebook

TERESA OF ÁVILA WAS
CANONIZED A SAINT IN
1622 BY POPE GREGORY
XV. IN 1970 POPE PAUL VI
NAMED SAINT TERESA OF
ÁVILA THE FIRST WOMAN
DOCTOR OF THE CHURCH.

Joy
Humility
Compassion
Generosity

These are just some of the qualities of the saints you'll find in our popular Encounter the Saints series. Join Saint Teresa of Ávila, Saint Thérèse of Lisieux, Saint Edith Stein, and many other holy women and men as they discover and try to do what God asks of them. Experience the challenges and holiness of the Church's heroines and heroes while encountering the saints in a new and fun way!

Collect all the Encounter the Saints books by visiting www.pauline.org.

Saint Edith Stein
Blessed by the Cross
by Mary Lea Hill, FSP

Saint Teresa of Ávila
Joyful in the Lord
by Susan Helen Wallace, FSP

Saint Thérèse of Lisieux
The Way of Love
by Mary Kathleen Glavich, SND

Visit www.jclubcatholic.org for lots of cool stories and activities just for you!

For My Friends

Jesus, you gave me the gift of my friends. Their friendship and love remind me of your love and faithfulness. Thank you for my friends. Help me to be a good friend to each of them. Teach me to be someone who listens, serves, and loves. Let all of my friendships be modeled on my relationship [...] me always to remember [...] Amen.

80

For All Children

Jesus, you said, "Let the little children come to me." I pray for all children of the world: for those in my school, in my town, [...] but also for those in all [...]

Dear and Sweet Mother Mary

Dear and sweet Mother Mary, keep your holy hand upon me; guard my mind, my heart, and my senses, that I may never commit sin. Sanctify my thoughts, affections, words, and actions, so that I may please you and your Jesus, my God, and [...] Mary.

Hail, Holy Queen

Hail, holy Queen, Mother of Mercy, our life, our sweetness, and our hope. To you do we cry, poor banished children of Eve; to you do we send up our sighs, mourning and weeping in this valley of tears. Turn then, most gracious advocate, your eyes of mercy toward us, and after this our exile, show unto us the blessed fruit of your womb, Jesus. O clement, O loving, O sweet Virgin Mary.

30

Prayers for Young Catholics is a book of basic and more advanced prayers. Beautifully expressed through artwork, it explains the importance of prayer and provides instruction on how to pray.

For young Catholics ages 8–12.

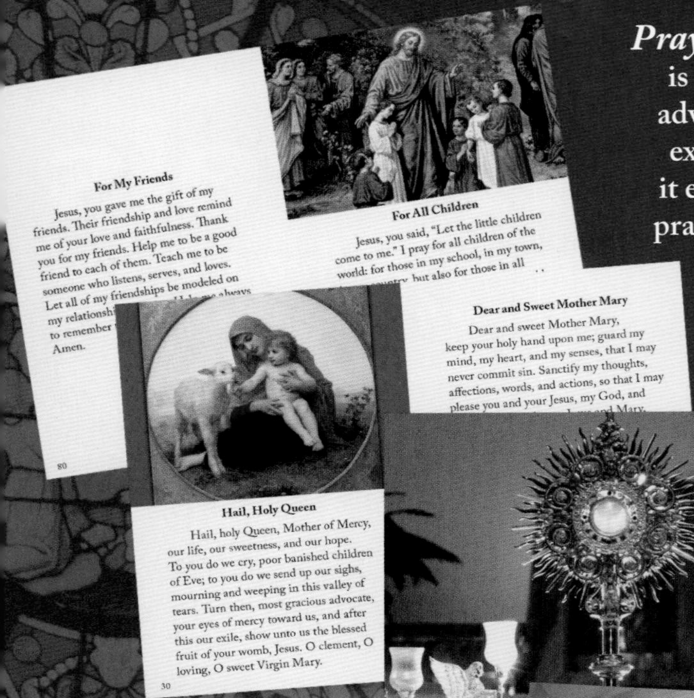

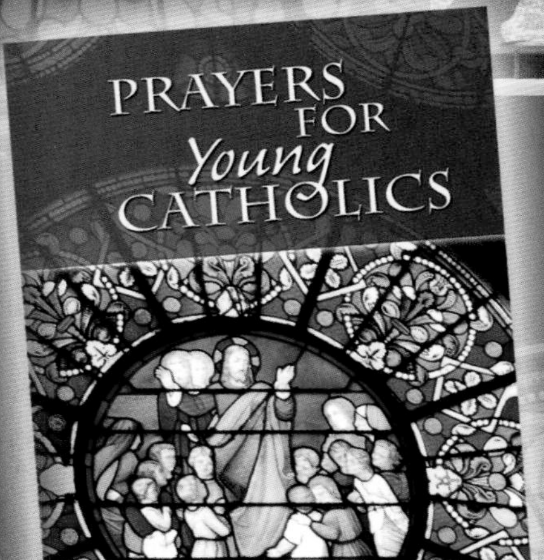

OUR CATHOLIC FAITH

PRAYERS FOR *Young* CATHOLICS

PRAYERS TO MARY

ISBN: 0-8198-5995-8 $14.95

Features & Benefits:

�֎ Offers a presentation page for gift givers

✖ Contains original prayers that are reflective of children's needs

✖ Ideal gift for young Catholics, 1st Communion, birthdays, and more

A Catholic Place for Kids

Your school may have hosted a JClub Catholic Book Fair. But did you know that you can go to

www.jclubcatholic.org

for stories, games, saints, activities, prayers, and even jokes?

JClub is where faith and fun are friends.

Who are the Daughters of St. Paul?

We are Catholic sisters. Our mission is to be like Saint Paul and tell everyone about Jesus! There are so many ways for people to communicate with each other. We want to use all of them so everyone will know how much God loves us. We do this by printing books (you're holding one!), making radio shows, singing, helping people at our bookstores, using the Internet, and in many other ways.

Visit our website at www.pauline.org

BOOKS & MEDIA

The Daughters of St. Paul operate book and media centers at the following addresses. Visit, call, or write the one nearest you today, or find us at www.pauline.org.

CALIFORNIA
3908 Sepulveda Blvd, Culver City, CA 90230 — 310-397-8676
3250 Middlefield Road, Menlo Park, CA 94025 — 650-369-4230

FLORIDA
145 S.W. 107th Avenue, Miami, FL 33174 — 305-559-6715

HAWAII
1143 Bishop Street, Honolulu, HI 96813 — 808-521-2731

ILLINOIS
172 North Michigan Avenue, Chicago, IL 60601 — 312-346-4228

LOUISIANA
4403 Veterans Memorial Blvd, Metairie, LA 70006 — 504-887-7631

MASSACHUSETTS
885 Providence Hwy, Dedham, MA 02026 — 781-326-5385

MISSOURI
9804 Watson Road, St. Louis, MO 63126 — 314-965-3512

NEW YORK
115 E. 29th Street, New York City, NY 10016 — 212-754-1110

TEXAS
Currently no book center; for parish exhibits or outreach evangelization, contact: 210-569-0500, or SanAntonio@paulinemedia.com, or P.O. Box 761416, San Antonio, TX 78245

SOUTH CAROLINA
243 King Street, Charleston, SC 29401 — 843-577-0175

VIRGINIA
1025 King Street, Alexandria, VA 22314 — 703-549-3806

CANADA
3022 Dufferin Street, Toronto, Ontario, Canada M6B 3T5 — 416-781-9131

SMILE
God loves you